PRINCESS

Ted Staunton

Red Deer Press

Northern Lights Young Novels are published by
Red Deer Press
813 MacKimmie Library Tower
2500 University Drive N.W.
Calgary Alberta Canada T2N 1N4

Credits
Edited for the Press by Peter Carver
Cover art and illustrations by Susan Gardos
Cover design by Duncan Campbell
Text design by Dennis Johnson
Printed and bound in Canada by Friesens for Red Deer Press

Acknowledgments
Financial support provided by the Canada Council, the Department of Canadian Heritage, the Alberta Foundation for the Arts, a beneficiary of the Lottery Fund of the Government of Alberta, and the University of Calgary.

National Library of Canada Cataloguing in Publication Data
Staunton, Ted, 1956–
Princess
(The kids from Monkey Mountain; #4)
ISBN 0-88995-242-6
I. Gardos, Susan. II. Title. III. Series: Staunton, Ted, 1956– Kids from Monkey Mountain; #4.
PS8587.T334P74 2001   jC813'.54   C2001-910693-9   PZ7.S8076Pr 2001

5 4 3 2 1

For Margaret, Aretha and Madeline

Chapter 1

My name is Mary Elizabeth Louise Harvey. I live at 43 Princess Street, Hope Springs, Ontario, Canada, The World. I forget the code. My family is my mom Donna Louise Harvey and our cat Lauren Bacall. Donna is very beatuful. Also my Gram and Grampa but they dont' live with us. My best friends are Lindsey and Tiffany. We love horses. My best thing from summer was going to Gram and Grampa's cottage and when I went to day camp with Lindsey and Tiffany. Then I had to stop because Travis Bee gave everybody head lice. Here is a picture of Donna and Lauren Bacall. Donna was almost on TV. She went to TV school until something happened.

P.S. I am called Mary Beth.

P.P.S. I mean my Gram and Grampa are my family not that they are beatuful. They are nice but wrinkly.

5

From Mr. Yates: Hi, Mary Beth. Welcome to Room 9!
I wish you were in the picture, too.

Friday, September 9

I like Ralph. He is the biggest cuddly bear I ever saw. It was cool that you won him at last years fall fair. I liked sitting with him for silent reading. Its like being on our couch with Lauren Bacall but softer and and no claws. I hope I win a bear at the fall fair. My mom says I have to be in the talent show. I have to say a poem. I wish Ralph purred.

Monday, September 11

Im glad you moved our seats. It is boring sitting right beside Travis who makes disgusting fart noises on purpose all day long. He is the worst boy. Some of the others are ok like Nick and Steve and Jeff. They are ok for boys. Ryan is sometimes ok. Travis Bee is a turkey. I promise I will not talk with Tiff and Lins too much unless I really need to. This is a picture of Ralph squashing A BOY.

Wedensday, September 13

At 5 after school I start dance class again. I go to Sodaberg School Of Dance. It is above Weclips Haircutters. We call Mrs. Sodaberg Mrs Dodobird. She looks birdy when she hops around. There is choir after that. Donna says I have to because you get poy poise. That is walking as if you are a princess so people notice you. That is why I have to wear dresses so much. I don't want to get noticed. If I was a princess I would be beatuful and have poise. Then I could wear jeans and ride my own horse. I would not care if anybody noticed or not.

From Mr. Yates: I think you have lots of poise already.

Thursday, September 14

Lindsey Tiffany and me are all going to be in the fashion show at this year's fair! It is fifteen days away. That is fun becuase all you do is walk and be poy poised and everybody just looks at the clothes not you. Lindsey saw the clothes already. There are really cool jeans that I can ask to wear and you maybe get to keep them. Expect for the talent show it will be sweet. The talent show will be pukey. Best will be the HORSE SHOW. This is Ralph at the HORSE SHOW. I just won him at a game.

Friday, Sept. 15

Today I have butterfly clips in my hair. If Travis tries to bug them he will get one noogie for every freckle on his face. My mom got them for me. If I want I can wear them for the talent show when I say my poem. I don't want to wear anything when I say my poem. That is becuase I don't want to say my poem, not becuase I want to be bare-naked. I dont' want to wear my dresses any more either. They are ridiculous. That is why I am having a SECRET MEETING at recess with T and L. Watch carefully. I have a plan.

Chapter 2

"Pass the gravy please, hon. More peas? Goodness, Mary Beth, that's a nice dress. Did we get that for you? You should wear that in the fashion show." Gram plunked herself down at the table, still wearing her apron. "How's the roast? Tell me, now. Did you get bread? What's this movie tonight? You know . . ."

Mary Beth sat in her grandparents' dining room. She was wearing her sky blue dress with puffy shoulders and white trim. She watched Grampa pour gravy onto his plate. Not too much, she hoped; she needed the gravy for her plan. When Gram stopped talking she swallowed and said, "It's called *Ants In Your Pants*. It's a cartoon, but with computers."

"Ants in your pants? Oh my." Gram wiggled at the thought. She was a hefty lady; the flesh on her arms jiggled. They were good hugging arms.

Mary Beth watched Grampa pass the gravy to her

mom. Donna took just a little and passed it to Gram, who chattered on. "Thanks, hon. Reminds me of the time we rented that cottage. They had a bird bath by the outdoor biffy . . ."

Grampa smiled and nodded, partly because that was all you needed to do when Gram got rolling and partly because he was a little deaf from his job at the car plant. Gram, on the other hand, was a clerk at the Hope Springs town hall. She chatted with everyone all day long, which gave her more to chat about when she came home.

Gram took a serving of gravy that went with her size, then passed the boat to Mary Beth. "Need some help, hon?"

"No, thanks." Mary Beth waited until Gram had resumed her story. She flicked her eyes left, right. No one was watching. Deliberately, she poured gravy on her meat, her potatoes, and her blue dress. It was hotter than she'd expected. "Yow!" she jumped, spilling more on herself. Still, it made a spectacular brown splotch across the cloudless blue. Donna and Gram leaped into action with cold water, tea towels, and the damp dish rag. Mary Beth held the dress wide for them and looked at Grampa as they scrubbed. His eye twitched in what could have been a wink. Mary Beth felt herself blush. Grampa took more potato.

"You can't go to the show like this," Donna groaned. "We'll have to go home first."

"Accidents happen," Gram said, sitting down again with a sigh. "There's apple pie for dessert."

Lauren Bacall looked up from the couch as they hurried in. She stretched and padded hopefully to her food bowl, but Donna bustled on past to run some cold water to soak the dress in. Mary Beth ran happily to her room. Step One of her plan had worked; she had a lot more mishaps lined up for the future, though preferably with cooler foods. Ketchup, for example, would be a natural. Or grape juice. It would take awhile to work through her whole dressing-up wardrobe, but she figured she could do it. Right now, though, it was almost movie time, which meant it was time for Step Two: comfy clothes. She took off the damaged dress and pulled on jeans and a sweatshirt with cats printed on it.

"See?" she said to Lauren Bacall, who had followed her. "That's you." She pointed to a black cat on her shirt. Lauren Bacall looked at her and meowed, then went back to her food bowl.

Mary Beth carried the dress to the bathroom, where her mom put it in the tub. "There." Donna stood up, sweeping auburn hair back from her forehead. Mary Beth wasn't exaggerating when she said her mom was beautiful. Donna turned and saw her daughter's clothes. "Aw, hon—"

"There wasn't time to choose," Mary Beth protested, already scooting down the hall. She stopped at the front door to pull on her runners. "And anyway, it's not school. It's just a movie. It'll be dark."

"Yes, but you never know—"

When someone might notice, Mary Beth finished in her head. As usual, she interrupted with, *"You're* not dressed up."

As usual, her mom replied, "You don't need to be noticed at Wilmot's Stationery."

You mean, you don't have to dress up if you're beautiful, Mary Beth thought. She was sure that was the real answer. She had to dress up all the time. Mary Beth's next line was always, "Well, I don't want to be noticed either." Now, though, Donna said, "Never mind." Her key was already in the lock. "We've got to go or we'll be late."

Mary Beth knew she should be happy as they drove to the mall. Step Two had worked; she was in her favorite clothes. Still, all this planning had left her a little on edge, and a clothes argument always made her feel bruised, regardless of whether she won or lost. It wasn't fun to argue with your mom.

And it wasn't as if clothes were all she and Donna disagreed about. Lately they argued over everything: breakfast cereal, choir, dance lessons, poise, and why

owning a horse was not a big possibility. Not to men-
tion the fall fair's talent show, which loomed like a
gigantic, pink, stain-proof dress with an extra-lacy
hem. How was she ever going to recite "MacAvity the
Mystery Cat" in front of everybody? With all the acting
and actions Donna wanted? Mary Beth sighed and
slumped deeper into the passenger seat of their ancient
Toyota.

Donna broke the silence. "The Plate Lady came in
today. There's a new one." Mary Beth perked up slight-
ly, in spite of herself. The Plate Lady collected plates
with pictures of Elvis on them, which she ordered
through the store. She had a hundred and two.

"What is it this time?" she asked.

"Scooter Elvis."

"*Scooter* Elvis?"

"Don't ask. He's wearing shades and skater shorts
and riding a scooter, no hands. I think they copied
Surfer Elvis and painted some clothes on him."

"Is it as good as Leprechaun Elvis?"

"Princess, *nothing* is as good as Leprechaun Elvis."

For the rest of the drive Donna joked about people who had come in the store that day. Mary Beth felt
her bad mood dissolve like a stain in the wash. It was
Movie Tuesday, their favorite night. She was wearing

her jeans. She knew her mom liked talking like this as much as she did. Donna should have been on TV, the way she'd wanted to be, Mary Beth thought as her mom mugged like a grumpy customer. She should have been an actress. She imagined Donna's face gigantic on a movie screen, imagined her at TV school. But things had happened, things nobody expected. Mary Beth's mood darkened. Then she heard Donna saying, "And inside the card there's this little line and underneath it says, 'Here's the straight poop: Happy Birthday.'"

She thought of the movie. She thought about horses and rides at the fall fair. She thought about her friends and the fashion show. She remembered Grampa's maybe wink. She'd do Step Three of her plan tomorrow. Mary Beth laughed. She felt terrific.

Chapter 3

Last night we saw Ants In Your Pants. *We always go to Tuesday movies because it is cheaper. Ralph would really like this movie. Its funny. The only way to make it better would be have horses. The best part was when Bud the Ant got stuck in the fat guys big hairy belly button at the beach and he yelled "GET ME OWDA HE AW!" and the guy burps and Bud went flying and lands on the ladys' you-knows and she screamed. Please I hope there is no home-work becuase I am going to Tiffs after school. We are prac-ticing our poise because the fair is only 9 days from now. I can hardly wait for it especially the HORSES except for the talent show which spoils everything. I have to practice for it, too. And I have dance at 5 and choir at church at 7. And and we have to do more of my PLAN. Right now I am wearing my yellow dress but watch later!! So please please PLEASE no homework and can I do silent reading with Ralph today.*

Mary Beth stopped to sharpen her pencil. It was the fourth time since she'd started writing. She smeared the shavings on the lap of her dress, then wrote more:

See how sharp my pencil just got? That's becuase of my Bud The Ant pencil sharpener that I got. Its on my desk. I will show you it because it is so cool. The way his arms and legs wave is like he is boogying. My mom got it at work but she kept it secret until after we saw the movie. She gets lots at work becuase she's worked there so long. Before she was at school to be on TV until something happened. This is Bud Boogying.

She stopped again and looked around. Tiff was writing. Lins was staring into space. Nick and Jeff were writing. Travis was aiming a spitball at Ryan's head. Mary Beth nudged him just in time. After that, except for sharpening breaks, Mary Beth spent the rest of journal time with her tongue clamped between her teeth, drawing the boogying Bud. She wanted it to be good. Mr. Yates had already suggested that she enter a picture in the art show at the fall fair.

As Mr. Yates collected the journals, she pulled a bag from her desk and asked to go to the washroom. There hadn't been time for this before. Mary Beth had already made a mental note to get to school earlier tomorrow.

In the privacy of one of the stalls, she opened the bag and took out a pair of shorts and a T-shirt advertising beer. She changed clothes, crumpling her pencil-marked dress into the bag. The shorts, which belonged to Tiffany, fit perfectly. The T-shirt, which belonged to Tiffany's brother, fit more like a tent.

Feeling comfortably sloppy, she returned to class. Lindsey and Tiffany grinned. Except for Travis Bee, who always stared at her (just to bug her, she was sure), nobody paid any attention at all. *Yes–s–s–s–s,* she thought. The clothes switcheroo was a trick she'd thought up for day camp, back in the summer, and then forgotten about when Donna sent her to her aunt's instead. Now, Lins and Tiff were helping by sometimes bringing clothes. This cut down the risk that Donna might catch her smuggling her own. With time to change back and forth, she could be princess-dress free at school—except for class picture day, of course. This was Step Three: her whole plan was working.

After school was as busy as Mary Beth thought it would be. Her first stop was Tiffany's house. Back in her dress again, she and her friends practiced walking with poise. This was more difficult than it seemed. The

living room was crowded with a baby grand piano and a pile of horse books no one wanted to move, and Lindsey's brand new platform sandals kept tripping her up. Besides which, the girls couldn't stop giggling. Finally Lindsey kicked off her shoes and threw up her hands.

"This is stupid. We've got to do something else."

"Like what?"

"Let's just all run out," Tiff said.

"Then nobody will see the clothes. We have to do something."

"We could dance," Mary Beth suggested, Sodaberg's already on her mind.

"Dance how?"

"*Dance* dance." She jumped up and down. "Boogie like Bud."

"Yeah, to 'Late Late'!" Lindsey said. "They play it and we run out and dance."

"And then," Tiff paused as the idea took shape, "at the end we all whinny and rear back and yell, 'Horses rule!'"

"*Swe–e–e–e–e–t!*"

They practiced. There was a lot more giggling.

Her mom pulled up in the Toyota just before five. Mary Beth suffered through her hour at Sodaberg School of Dance, where nobody boogied like Bud. They had a sandwich supper at home. Then Mary Beth put on her jeans and sweatshirt again. She was allowed to dress this way for choir practice. Donna said she didn't ever have to dress up for rehearsal.

Mary Beth wasn't any crazier about choir than she was about dance class. How could anybody be when the choir included Travis, whose dad, Reverend Bee, was the minister at the church? On the other hand, there was no dressing up, and Miss Cousins, the choirmistress, was nice.

Workmen were going in and out as they got to the church. Part of the building was being fixed. Mary Beth saw Nick's dad, who was in charge, talking with Reverend Bee. As they got out of their car, Miss Cousins pulled in beside them. "Hi, hi!" Donna called. The grown-ups chatted their way across the parking lot. Mary Beth followed a step behind, listening. Miss Cousins was shaped something like Gram, only younger. Unlike Gram, she never said more than she had to.

"Have you decided what to do for the ceremony?" Donna asked.

"Mmmm. Two songs and a solo," Miss Cousins answered. "Short and sweet."

Uh-oh, Mary Beth thought. She'd forgotten that the junior choir had to do something special on Sunday. Now she knew what would be coming next.

"Well," Donna said as they entered the church, "I

mean, forgive me, pushy mom and all, but a solo would be such a great experience for Mary Beth. You know, I think she just needs a little encouragement, and . . ."

Oh no, Mary Beth thought, dropping back, then stopping by the workmen's scaffold. *No, no, no.* It was *so* embarrassing; Donna always did this. Mary Beth didn't know much about singing, but she figured she knew if she was a good singer or not. She knew she wasn't. Fortunately, it seemed Miss Cousins knew that, too, because she always found a way to avoid Donna's suggestions. It was one of the reasons Mary Beth liked her.

There was a crash behind her. Mary Beth started, then whirled. Travis stood grinning, a dropped hammer at his feet.

"Why do you *do* things like that?" She forced the words through her annoyance.

"Because it's *fu–u–un.*"

Mary Beth shook her head and walked off. Miss Cousins was starting the practice. As the music began, Donna called from the front pew, "Don't slouch, Mary Beth honey." Mary Beth slouched more. Down the row, Travis was trying to flick boogers at her. She was going to have to do something about him, Mary Beth thought. She sighed as she sang. Sometimes there seemed to be so much to do.

Chapter 4

My pencil will be this sharp all day becuase of Bud. I am putting him up on my desk so I can remember to boogie at the fashion show. I hope Lins does not fall off her platforms. Even if she does we will still be better than saying my poem. At least I do not have to sing on Sunday. (Miss Cousins told me in secret.) Have you seen that I am not in dresses all day hint hint becuase my plan is working perfectly. Can I please do silent reading with Ralph today because I did not get to yesterday. Even though I asked?

From Mr. Yates: Boogie at the fashion show? Sing? Miss Cousins? Bud is neat. Everybody has to have a turn sitting with Ralph, remember? I also noticed your new clothes, especially your shirt! I didn't know you drank that brand of beer.

Friday, September 22

I did a picture for the fair like you said. It is of Bud the Ant flying through the air off the guys belly only he is going to land on a horse instead of the ladys you knows. Maybe if I win a prize for it I will not have to do my poem. I hope so because the fair is next weekend and I do not know it good enough yet and mom says I can only go to sleepover at Lins tonight if I practice first. It is a good thing Bud's head is easy to draw. Becuase since Travis broke it off it keeps rolling over face down when you lay it on the desk. Thank you for being mad with him yesterday. I was mad when he wrecked my sharpener. He is going to get it.

P.S. I DO NOT drink beer. The shirt was Tiffs brothers. That was why it was so big. My today shirt is mine. It has cats on it. The black cat is just like Lauren Bacall. My stupid poem for the talent contest is about a cat too. Really it is not the poem that is stupid it is the CONTEST.

Monday, September 25

I have a new Bud The Ant sharpener. It is just like the old one that Travis broke last Thursday expect it is not broken. I am not leaving it on the desk any more though in case he gets itchy fingers again the next time I am sitting with Ralph. He gave it to me (Travis not Ralph haha) at the end of church yesterday. That was after I got him becuase I was so mad at him for breaking Bud and bugging me. I didn't tell anybody except the jr. choir so I would not get stopped. Last time at church Travis pretended to break an egg on my head. So yesterday guess what I did. I stuck an egg down his underpants right before he had to sing the solo. It got all over everything even on the new Bud. I know he did that on purpose. He is a jerk. I am sorry but he is. Anyway I washed it. Now I can do my usual plan and practice for fashion show becuase the fair is here this weekend. I can hardly wait for the rides and the HORSES. I will watch all day and maybe forget to do my poem unless I win a picture prize and dont' have to.

From Mr. Yates: I'm glad you did a picture; I'll look for it at the fair. What poem are you reciting?

Tuesday, September 26

Last night was fashion show practice and we got our clothes. I get to wear bell jeans and a stripe top and guess

26

what they will let us dance like we want! The only thing different is at the end we have to stand still while they tell what we are wearing. Everybody thought it was so cool. Especially when we whinnied except Lins fell off her platforms again. We went in Lins's van. It is nicer than our car. Her family is rich. but it is the same as ours too (expect for her little brother) because Lins's dad has gone away. Expect Lins knows her dad and mine I don't' because he went away when I was not even born. I think he lives in Vancouver. And also Lins's's mom said she wanted to get out of the city after she had kids but Donna said that shes always wanted to get out of here. I do not want to get out of here. I think we get to keep the clothes. I know almost my whole poem but not my gestures. The poem is called Macavity The Mystery Cat. Do you like my shirt?

From Mr. Yates: The show sounds great. I know the poem. Maybe I will read it to the class. As I told you, the word on your shirt is not for school.

Wednesday, September 27

Thank you for writing Wednesday on the board. It is the

only thing good that has happened since Donna came early yesterday. I forgot I had to go to the dentist. I don't think she needed to get that mad. It was her shirt. I guess you see I am all dressed up again. I didn't do my poem very well and we didn't go to a movie and the fair is this weekend. I will have to make a new plan.

Chapter 5

Donna was in the car when Mary Beth came out of Sodaberg's School of Dance. "How'd it go?" she asked as they pulled away. "Did you get that tricky bit?"

"Kind of," Mary Beth said. Really she hadn't gotten it at all.

"Way to go." Donna shifted gears. "It was tough when I was there, too."

Yeah, right, thought Mary Beth. Mrs. Sodaberg always said Donna had been her best pupil ever. "Such a hard worker!" Well, thought Mary Beth, she was a hard worker, too, just at different things, like drawing horses or avoiding princess clothes. And she'd work even harder if she was learning something useful, like riding.

"No choir tonight," Donna said. Mary Beth felt a flicker of hope.

"We're staying home to practice for the show." The hope flickered out.

At home, Mary Beth put on shorts and a sweat-shirt. They had supper, then began practicing. It was slow going. "Macavity the Mystery Cat" was a long, humorous poem, by T.S. Eliot, about a cat who was a master criminal. Mary Beth usually knew the words, but it was tough remembering the actions and expressions Donna wanted her to use. Donna could do it perfectly. After four tries at the stealing the jewels part, Mary Beth went to the kitchen for a glass of water.

"Princess, it's just not that hard," Donna's voice followed her. "Just pretend to stroke your whiskers with one paw and hold the necklace up with the other and do the crafty smile."

"But I stink at being a cat." She turned on the tap. She didn't really want a drink, but the running water drowned out her mom's reply. Mary Beth turned off the tap. "Why don't *you* say it instead of me?" she called. It wasn't the first time she'd thought this, but it was the first time she'd said it.

"Because it's mainly a show for kids. Besides, we've worked hard on this, and it'll be good for you."

"But I'm already in the fashion show, and the tal-ent show is right in the middle of the horse show, and you said—"

"I know what I said. You can watch all the rest. Now, let's try it again."

Mary Beth tried again. She forgot to stroke her whiskers. She tried again. She forgot the words. She tried again. She dropped the necklace. She tried again. She forgot the crafty smile *and* the words. "I hate this," she said. She flopped on the couch, narrowly missing Lauren Bacall, who scrambled out of the way.

"You won't when everyone claps."

"Yes, I will."

"No, you won't. Trust me; You'll like it when they notice."

"But I don't *want* to be noticed."

"You will."

"No, I won't and I stink at this!"

"No, you don't! And you won't, either, if you listen to me. You'll be great."

"I don't want to be great!"

Donna looked hard at her. "Listen. Is this asking so much? Do you know how much I do for you? How much Gram and Grampa sacrifice for you so you can dress nicely and take lessons and get out of here like I never could?"

"I don't even want to *take* lessons. I never said I did. All I want is a horse, and I don't want to move away anyway." Mary Beth was scared and angry at the same time.

Donna's lips pinched white. "You will, Missy. Just you wait and see. You'll want to get out of here so bad, just the way I did—"

"*Then why didn't you go?*" Mary Beth shouted. She knew it was a terrible mistake as soon as the words were out.

"I think you know," her mother said fiercely. Suddenly Donna looked as if she were about to cry. Mary Beth couldn't breathe. She knew why Donna hadn't gone. She'd had a baby right after high school—an unexpected baby whose father ran away. She'd named the baby Mary Elizabeth Louise.

Then her mom was on the couch beside her, hugging her.

"That wasn't your fault," she was saying. "Every day I'm glad you're here." Mary Beth hugged back and started to cry. They were still hugging when the telephone rang. It was Lindsey.

Mary Beth listened, sniffling. Then she covered the phone with her hand.

"Can I g–go to rides night at the fair tomorrow with Lins and Tiff?" It was still hard to talk. It wasn't an easy question, either. Rides night was the beginning of

the fair, when only the midway was open. It was expensive, unless you had a pass. Donna smiled. Her face was tear streaked. She opened her purse and held something up. "Your pass. Tell Lindsey I'll drive. Then let's try Macavity again."

"Do you think he's going to make it?" Nick asked.

"No way," Tiffany said as she and Ryan staggered up.

"I hope not," Mary Beth muttered to Lindsey. It was rides night. They were standing in front of the Gravitwirl, a spinning ride. Travis had bet everyone he could go on it ten times in a row without throwing up. Donna was over by the skeeball booth, chatting with Nick's mom and Jeff's dad. Lights and music mingled with the aroma of French fries.

"Who's up?" someone said. They were taking turns on the ride to make sure Travis didn't cheat. He'd already tried to sneak off once. Ryan and Tiffany had just finished numbers six and seven.

"We are," said Lindsey. Mary Beth hurried up the steps after her. Ride number eight was about to begin.

Inside, Travis was looking a little pale, but he managed to make a face and lean toward them. The girls rolled their eyes. "You're just pretending," Lindsey said. She was right. Travis wasn't really sick until ride number nine. Then he threw up more than Mary Beth thought a person could possibly hold, just about everywhere the Gravitwirl could spin him. The shrieking started before the machine stopped. Passengers spilled off.

As they ran, Mary Beth called, "Hey, Lins! I think I know how to get out of the talent show."

Chapter 6

Friday, September 29

I have made a really cool plan with Lins and Tiff. I am
going to be sick as soon as we finish the fashion show becuase
the talent show is right after it and mom said she would get
me to go on first so I will not miss too much of the horse
jumping. But if I am sick I will have to go right outside and
get fresh air and then I will not miss any of it AND I WILL
NOT HAVE TO SAY MACAVITY THE MYSTERY CAT
AT ALL and it will not be my fault. Of course I will not
really be sick just pretending. We are making some fake barf
out of cotton candy and caramel corn we saved from last
night. After school we will mix it with mustard milk vini-
gar pickel relish and root beer. Tiff says we can do it at her
place. Tomorrow as soon as we finish I will pretend to sick
up all over my talent show clothes (a stupid dress) when my
mom is not watching. Then I will have to WEAR MY
FASHION SHOW CLOTHES AND REST AT THE
HORSE SHOW ALL AFTERNOON. Do you want to know

how we got the idea.? Here is a hint. This is Travis after nine times on the GRAVYT GRAVITWIRL (a ride where you spin around so fast they take the floor away).

P.S. The man that runs the ride was realy mad becuase Travis barfed inside. The ride. He had to help clean it up. It was gross.

P.P.S. Can I sit with Ralph today becuase I didn't win him at any games.?

Monday, Octrober 2

The fair was really really really really good. I got a 2nd place ribbon for my picture. It only got a little bit wet and the pigs didn't wreck it. We are going to put it up. I won a bear at ring toss. (he is not big like Ralph but he is still huggy so that is what I have called him. Huggy.) Gram got ribbons for best apple pie and best butter tarts. We got to eat some becuase they didn't get wet and the pigs didn't wreck them either. I went on every ride. We went on the Fairiss wheel at the very end of Sat. night after the demolishun derby. We saw the whole town up high. With all the lights it was like being up so high we were looking down at the stars. The horse show was SUPER SUPER good even though I got soaking and missed some of it becuase of the pigs. Lins and Tiff and me are going to start a horse club. We will make a scrapbook. We want to all take riding lessons together and save up and buy a horse together too. Everybody said we were best in the talent fashion show. It was funny when they got the music mixed up.

From Mr. Yates: What music got mixed up? How was the talent show? What happened with the pigs?

Tuesday, October 3

The best part about the pigs was when everybody chased them. They were very cute and squealy and I felt sorry for them even if it was funny at the same time. Then everybody got soaked and the fire trucks and ambuelances came. That was funny too. I bet it scared the horses though. Tonight we are going to the library and then wer'e going to see a movie Dancing Fools You. *Its very romantic about dancing but not the kind we do at dance class. Thank God. Here is one of the pigs. It was right beside somebodys backpack. I think Ryans.*

P.S. The music got mixed up just before us. When Mrs.

Guster split her pants. Grampa says he can see she is not losing any but I don't know what any.

From Mr. Yates: Where did the pigs come from? Did you use your plan?

Wesneday, Wednesday October 4

Last night we saw Dancing Fools You. *It was very good but boring with too much smooching. I did not beleive it at the end when the girl got to be a good dancer after all all of a sudden. That does not happen at Sodaberg School Of The Dance I can tell you. If you trip at the beginning you still trip at the end. If I were that girl I would have been a vet instead.*

P.S. I think the pigs came from somebodys farm. I already said about the talent show.

From Mr. Yates: I'm confused, Mary Beth. Could you tell the whole story about the pigs? I checked your journal and you have not told about the talent show—or your plan.

Thursday, October 5

I am sure I told this but OK here goes. Right before the talent show me and mom were at the stage and everybody was there waiting except Travis I think but Ryan was there becuase they were going to do a comedy act. And mom was saying the jewls part for me again. And then this lady Mrs. Goodenuf started talking to her. And then Ryan said hey look and all of a sudden this baby pig ran by. And then there was this big crash over by the art show. And then a big pig ran by. And then there was this big crash over by the baking contest. And then another baby pig ran by again with these people chasing it. And then people were yelling and running around all over the place. The chairs in front of the stage got crashed over. And then DING DING DING the fire alarm goes off and all of a sudden there is water sprinkling all over the place and screaming and all of us ran outside. I got soaked. The fire trucks and ambuelances came. Everybody said the pigs got out of a pen by the animal petting place but no one knows how. Ryan said the last pig they caught was snuffing in Traviss' backpack. So there was no talent show. In case you are wandering I was not going to use my plan any way. I decided I didn't' need it after all. It was too much trouble and besides I was con-

fidet. Now I don't have to act any more. Im going to do HORSE CLUB scrapbook instead with Tiff and Lins. Can I sit with Ralph today because you didn't pick me last time.?

From Mr. Yates: Bravo!

Chapter 7

The very worst thing in the world has happened. Mom says that becuase I liked the fashion show so much and becuase I missed the talent show I have to oddition for a play called All Of Her. *It is on Thursday. I can say my poem. I have to sing and dance too. I hate shows. It is not fair. We cannot afford to go to the movie tonight because we have to take Lauren Bacall to the vet for her shots. It is a stupid movie anyway. I hate movies too.*

From Mr. Yates: The show is called Oliver. It's a story by a famous author named Charles Dickens. I heard that the Hope Springs Players are putting it on. I bet you'll have fun. You just told me you were confident, remember?

Wesday, Oct. 11

I don't feel like writing today.

From Mr. Yates: Oliver has a lot of parts for kids. Maybe some friends would like to audition, too.

(written by Mary Beth) *HA HA*

Thursday October 12

~~*I have a plan for the odd audition. I still have my fake barf and I will use it tonight. I will barf it all over everything on the stage and I will sneak moms bad word t shirt there too and wear it becuase*~~ *you never dress up for rehearsal and I will have to go home and I don't want to go to Dodobird School of Dance. I don't want to say my cat poem Im sick of it I stink at it I told a lie I was not confidet at the talent show. That was not why I did not do my plan. Really I left the fake barf at home by accident so I couldnt do it. I was scared. I was so scared I probably couldnt have done it anyway. I am tired of plans. Lins says*

*she is going to try out too but I still don't want to go
tonight. I want to stay home with Huggy and Lauren
Bacall and draw HORSES. I don't know what to do.*

**From Mr. Yates: I know you'll do your best. Let me
know what happens.**

Chapter 8

Travis was yodeling and riding a tricycle down the crowded hall as Mary Beth and Donna stepped into the church basement. *HEE–YUK–YUK–YUK.* Travis's laugh grated behind him as he trundled by, knees up to his ears.

"He's too big for that," complained a grown-up voice. *Not in the brains department,* thought Mary Beth. She didn't want to waste any energy on Travis tonight; she had more important things to do. Beneath the cardigan she carried was a plastic container filled with the mixture she and her friends were calling fake barf. She'd kept it hidden in the back of their cluttered refrigerator ever since. It looked as if tonight would be the time to use it.

A lady stood by the stairs, handing file cards to people as they headed up to the sanctuary.

"What are they for?" Mary Beth asked.

"You put your name and number on them," Donna said, "and the part you want. Then they have a list."

The sanctuary had far more people in it than it did on Sundays. Donna led them to a seat in the middle. Mary Beth put her sweater and her secret burden down on the pew beside her, and looked around. Bud the Ant's voice echoed in her head: *Get me owdah heah!* Mr. Yates must have been right about there being lots of parts for kids: there were tons of them here. She saw kids from dance class and kids from choir and kids from day camp. From Room Nine alone she spotted Nick, Stephanie, and Ryan. And there was Lindsey with her mom, near the back. They waved.

There was a call for everyone's attention. Mary Beth turned and recognized Mrs. Goodenough, the lady who had been backstage at the talent show, before the pig invasion. As she did, Travis slid into the pew beside her, a pop can in his hand. Mary Beth turned away.

"Good evening, everybody. Thanks for coming. I'm Anne Goodenough, the director." As Mrs. Goodenough explained how things would work, Mary Beth thought about how and when she'd put her plan into action. She'd have to get excused, go into the washroom maybe, make lots of noise, and come out choking and gagging with the fake barf all over her. It wasn't a comforting thought. Mary Beth had smelled it when she,

Tiff and Lindsey had mixed it. Since then, it had had two weeks to get worse: she didn't want to add any real throw-up on top of things. It occurred to her that doing all this might be a tougher acting job than simply doing the audition. Still, she thought, it would be worth it to escape being stared at on a stage.

A metallic clatter interrupted everything. Travis had dropped his empty can. People turned. Travis stared back blankly. Mary Beth leaned as far away from him as possible. Mrs. Goodenough cleared her throat and continued, gravel-voiced, "Please fill out your cards and carry them with you to your first station. Blue cards start with dance, yellow with voice, pink with readings. Five minutes, please."

Mary Beth turned to Donna, who handed her a blue card. For the first time, she noticed her mother was holding a yellow one. "Who's that for?"

"Me." Donna was busy filling in the card.

"You? You're trying out?"

"Mm-hm. Mrs. Goodenough asked me to. So I thought about it and I'm going to."

"Oh, swe—e—e—e—t!" Mary Beth said. She just knew Donna would be fantastic. "When did she ask you?"

"I'll tell you about it later. Let's get going."

Mary Beth's worries scattered like baby pigs at the fair. She leaped to her feet, almost hitting Travis. They shuffled past him into the crowded aisle. There were so many kids here, all wanting to be in the play: a bunch of them had to be more talented than she was. Even better, it didn't matter now what she did herself; her mom was going to be the star of the whole show. She'd be so busy she wouldn't mind at all if her daughter just sat and watched. Mary Beth wouldn't have to try. She wouldn't have to be nervous. She wouldn't have to pretend to throw up. Imagine, helping Donna learn *her* lines. It was a lovely thought that carried her all the way to her first station, silently clapping her hands. She didn't wonder where she'd left her cardigan and container until a long time later.

Chapter 9

Today is a Friday the 13th. Last night was OLIVER auditions. It was very surprising. Lins was there and Stef Ryan Nick and Travis too. Tiff did not go. She is too busy with piano. And guess who else tried out. I'll tell you. MY MOM. She was so terrific she is going to get a big part maybe Nancy for sure. Nancy is a beatuful lady in the play who dies of murder. But not till nearly the end. She said Mrs. Goodenough (who is the director) asked her to at the fall fair becuase she heard her saying my poem and thought she was excellent. (She was) You had to go to one room to sing and down to the basement to dance together and into the sankchewary to act. Only I did not have to say Macavity. You had to read lines from the play instead. I was supposed to be a boy in a big gang. (yuck). I was not very good. Donna says it will be fun to be in the play with my friends but not if I am no good. If she gets a part (SHE WILL) she will not care. Then I could go to practice and work on the horse scrapbook maybe. Nicks' mom who was there said she really really liked my picture I did that was in the fair. She said it should have been 1st place and she is a good artist. Remember when she did the mural with our class last year. Now she is going to paint the back pictures for on the stage. They will call on the weekend to say who got parts or not. Travis yelled a lot and flicked fake boogers at everybody. Just like always. Here is my beatuful mom saying her part.

Sunday, October 15

Donna answered the telephone. Mary Beth was in her room, cutting a picture of a pony out of a *National Geographic*. Lauren Bacall was curled up beside her. Soon they would be going to Gram and Grampa's for dinner.

"Hello?" Donna's voice carried down the hall. "Oh, *hi!*"

Mary Beth stopped to listen. "No problem," Donna said. Then she said, *"Really?* Thank-you, thank-you!" Mary Beth jumped up. Lauren Bacall darted under the bed.

"Yes!" Donna gushed. "I'm thrilled. It's a great

part!" Mary Beth was about to run down the hall, cheering, when her mother said, "Now, what about Mary Beth?" She froze. "Oh," Donna said abruptly. "Well, then, I don't think I can, after all. This was for Mary Beth; she'll be so disappointed."

What? Mary Beth thought.

"And, I mean, how could I arrange babysitting and—"

What was Donna doing? She could stay at Gram's, she could come along, she could— "Well, I thought her audition went very well," Donna's voice interrupted. "She's just as good as—"

How do you know, Mary Beth thought desperately. *You didn't even see me audition.* Things were going badly wrong.

"What do you mean, 'her attitude'?" Donna's voice sharpened. "She wants to be in this play a lot, believe me."

No I don't, no I don't, Mary Beth cried silently, clenching her fists.

"I can't tell her I'm going to be in it and she's not."

Yes you can, yes you can. Her nails were digging into the palms of her hands.

"Well, it doesn't have to be a big part." Donna said. "Just to get her feet wet. I mean, if her friends—"

There was a pause. "That would be *perfect.* Thank-you so much. I'm glad you understand. Yup, I'll mark the date down. Thanks again. Bye."

Mary Beth was sitting on the floor, pretending to look at the picture, when her mom came bustling in. "Guess who just called?" Donna said breathlessly. "Mrs. Goodenough. We've both got parts! And—she said you were fantastic!"

Thursday, November 2

"No, no, no," Mrs. Goodenough's voice rasped across the gym. "Never cross downstage in front of the star." Some of the grown-ups, including Donna, were rehearsing a scene. Over by the hallway, Ryan's mom and another lady were measuring people for costumes. At Mary Beth's end of the gym, Miss Toomey, who also taught at Sodaberg's, was showing all the kids a dance step. "Step, ball, change," she demonstrated, her warm-up pants swishing. Mary Beth, suffering, demonstrated with her. It wasn't that the step was hard; she'd done it a million times at Sodaberg's. What bothered her was standing out. This was the third rehearsal, and while nobody had yet mentioned that she wasn't good enough to be here, she was sure they knew. Which was too bad, because while the waiting could be boring, she'd found herself rather enjoying the organized confusion of other times, especially with her friends.

"Ready?" asked Miss Toomey. "Let's try it: two, three, and—" The group shuffled back and forth like an unruly amoeba.

"Break time," shouted Mrs. Goodenough, now standing in the middle of the gym. She was wearing a sweatshirt that read *BECAUSE I SAY SO*. Instantly everyone was laughing and talking. Kids dug out Hallowe'en candy. Mrs. Goodenough marched out for a cigarette.

"My leg still hurts," Lindsey complained. She and Mary Beth walked to the door. She'd hurt it trick-or-treating, tripping in her platform sandals as she, Mary Beth and Tiffany clomped off a porch, all crammed into a homemade horse costume. They'd all fallen, but Lindsey was the one they'd landed on.

Mary Beth pushed open the door. The nights were chilly now, but she'd already made a habit of stepping out at break time. It gave people less chance to notice her—unless they were out for a smoke.

"Mary Beth Harvey." It was a command. In Mrs. Goodenough's voice, everything was a command. Mary Beth knew instantly that somehow she'd failed, even at not being noticed. Without looking at Lindsey, she walked over. Mrs. Goodenough looked down at her through a haze of cigarette smoke. "Good dancing," she said. "Thanks for helping."

Mary Beth shrugged and looked away. "It's easy."

"Then tell me something: why don't you want to be in the show?"

Mary Beth looked up in surprise. She didn't know what to say. Mrs. Goodenough was waiting for an answer. At last, she said, "I know I'm really not good enough to be in."

"Who told you that?" Mrs. Goodenough squinted and drew on her cigarette.

"I heard my mom talk to you on the phone. She made you pick me."

"Sweetie," Mrs. Goodenough growled, "you misunderstood. I didn't say you weren't good. I said I didn't think you really wanted to be in the play."

"What?" Mary Beth said, even more surprised and tongue-tied. "Oh."

"You're good enough to be here. What I'm asking is, do you want to be?"

Mary Beth thought hard, or tried to. Her mind was a jumble of horses and movies and Donna. Scrapbooks jostled in the confusion with Gram and Grampa

and Lindsey and the others. Plans and organized confusion bobbed like Hallowe'en apples. She thought
about them all very fast while plumes of smoke drifted,
dragonlike, from Mrs. Goodenough's nose.

Then she said, "I didn't before, but now I think I
do. But I don't want to be a star actress when I grow
up."

"Fair enough; neither do I." Mrs. Goodenough
ground out her cigarette with the toe of her tennis shoe
and started back inside. "Now, let's go have some fun.
All right, everybody. Back to work!"

Chapter 10

Tuesday, November 7

*D*o you see what I am wearing today? My fashion show jeans. I am allowed to any day we are rehearsing becuase you never dress up for rehearsal. Mom says this is a rule. I wish we had rehearsal every day. Lins and I are taking our horse scrapbook for when there is waiting around.

Wednesday November 15

Last night at practice we stunk. All the gang kids I mean becu because we were goofing around. Mrs. Goodenough got very mad and yelled. She said we all had too much sugar at Halloween. We think she drinks too much coffee. She smokes a lot too. The boys are hopeless at dancing. I had to help them again becuase I know how from Sodabergs'. Mr. Yates this is a dumb question but you did not take my fake barf did you? I cant' find it anywhere and I can't remember if I brought it to school. Can I sit with Ralph today?

From Mr. Yates: I don't have it. I think you said you took it to your audition. And yes, as you know, you got to sit with Ralph.

Thursday November 16

Because becuase. There. I have practiced like you told me. Its' boring.

Friday, November 24

Tomorrow we are going to hear Tiff at her Christmas piano concert. It is why she cannot be in Oliver becu because she has to practice piano so much. Not only for the concert but all the time. Except she is really really good and wants to be a musician. I will not mind getting dressed up. because because becuase because because

Monday December 4

Tiff and Lins and I finished our first whole HORSE SCRAPBOOK. We are starting another one right away. The thing I want for Christmas is a horse.

We are going to ask for one altogether that we could share. Then we could take turns looking after it too. Every time I looked after it I would not have to get dressed up either. Because because because because because because.

Wednesday, December 13

Last night at practice we were getting good. Nick's mom has got a big backdrop all painted to look like the city London. It looks fantastic. She has another to do too. She showed me her plans. She is a terriffic artist. Here is London (sort of because I am not as good as her)

P.S. None of the girls thought it was funny when Travis did that thing with the water fountain. It is the wrong time of the year to get all wet. Besides he was aiming it to make it look like we wet our pants. It is true. This is very embarassing for everyone. He is a bozo.

Monday, January 8

*At Christmas we stayed home except for going to Gram
and Grampa's. I did not get a horse but guess what I did
get? A bear like Ralph. I am calling him Bogey. Donna
says that was the name of Lauren Bacall's husband. I
mean the actress Lauren Bacall not our cat Lauren Bacall
who she is named after. Because our cat Lauren Bacall
likes to snooze on top of my bear. I also got two books and
a CD and a video National Velvet and a game and a
sweatshirt and jeans from Grampa. Also a new sled. Lins
and Tiff and I went every day to Monkey Mountain.
Everybody was there. Travis got in everbodys way because
he kept on falling off his snowboard. He cannot board well
but he does excellent face plants. Here he is doing one.*

Friday, February 2

*Tonight is opening night for Oliver. Last night was dress
rehearsal. We are so good. Nobody forgot anything except
once. Are you going to come and see us?*

From Mr. Yates: You bet!

Monday, February 5

I saw you at Oliver Saturday. Your wife is pretty. You should have brought Ralph too. I bet you did not see me thanks to my makeup. If you can't guess which one was me I was the one with the raggedy striped pants. On Friday night they gave all the girls and ladies flowers but they didn't know which of us in the gang was even girls, that's how good the makeup was. Thank God. You should have heard them clap for my mom too. It was even more than last night. Now we have time off until Thursday night. I don not have to dress up though because it is time off. Next weekend we will do it all again then have a pizza party. Its fun. Im' tired although. No homework PLEASE.

Monday February 12

Saturday was closing night for Oliver and we had a big pizza party. At the party guess what happened? Nick's mom told my mom that I was really good at art and that if I was interested I should take some lessons and she told her a lady who teaches it. So I begged "Please can I take art instead of going to Sodabergs just to try it." Because I really really want to. Be an artist instead of an actor. So

mom said "but I thought you had fun." I said "I did but I like art better and I already tried plays like you wanted." So mom said to Nick's mom "Do you think it would be worth it?". She said "Absolutley. In fact, maybe next time Mary Beth could help with art for the play. It's going to be Charlotte's Web." And I said "Yay" because I love that book. So mom told Grampa and Gram and they said they were so proud of me from being in Oliver that they would pay for the lessons and I can still go to Sodabergs too because art will be on Wednesdays after dancing. That is kind of stinky but it means I can quit choir which is sweet. I have fingers and toes crossed all the time to make it happen. Here is me being a dancing artist and helping with Charlotte's Web. I specialize in horse pictures and am a vet in summer.

EXTRA IMPORTANT P.S. Remember my fake barf? I think I found it. This morning I saw a plastic jar just like the one it was in, only all frosty like it came from the freezer. Guess who'se desk it is in. Hint: he is A BOY. And guess what else? Artists do not dress up. I am glad. With barf around I think it is safer. Do you like my T-shirt?

Praise for Monkey Mountain books

"Chapter book readers will enjoy the pranks and predicaments friends and family face." –*Quill & Quire*

"Although these stories are fast-paced and funny, Staunton also digs deeply into his characters and makes us care about their anxieties and appreciate the ways they cope with their problems." –*City Parent*

"A cast of dynamic, memorable characters, plenty of humour (a Staunton trademark) and well-paced plots with believable school-age conflicts and satisfying endings. . . . The humour, conflict, and true-to-life dialogue will be enjoyed by all. . . . It's the stories themselves, and the well-defined characters that will keep readers on the lookout for more episodes in the lives of 'The Kids from Monkey Mountain.' Highly recommended." –*Canadian Materials*

Don't miss these other great books from the Kids at Monkey Mountain

Two False Moves

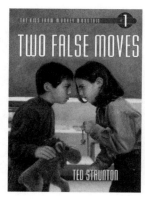

Nick can't shake off classroom competition from Lindsey, his arch enemy. For one thing, she hogs all the show-and-tell time. Far worse, however, is the fact that Lindsey's family might buy the house Nick's family is renting. The final stroke comes when Nick's teacher decides on partners for science projects and pairs him off with—you guessed it—Lindsey. By the time it's all over, Nick realizes that, despite all the advantages Lindsey seems to have, he may have a few blessings of his own.

Ages 7–10 • Grades 3–5 • ISBN 0-88995-205-1 paper • 8 B&W line drawings • CDN 6.95 • US 4.95 • UK £3.99

The Monkey Mountain Monster

Mouthy Mona is a put-down artist extraordinaire. Lindsey wants no part of it, but Mona has lured Lindsey's best friend, Caitlin, into her crowd of disciples—which leaves Lindsey out in the cold. On a dare Lindsey agrees to sleep out in her backyard. To make matters worse, the Ooly-Gooly monster is on the prowl. Can Lindsey fight off her fears—and the Ooly-Gooly—to make it through the night? When the monster finally shows up, chaos and panic set in with lively results.

Ages 7–10 • Grades 3–5 • ISBN 0-88995-206-X paper • 10 B&W line drawings • CDN 6.95 • US 4.95 • UK £3.99

Forgive Us Our Travises

Travis Bee is the youngest of three sons of Reverend Bee, one of Hope Spring's most respected citizens. Travis will go to any length to attract attention to himself, whether it's spraying the Sunday morning congregation with water, clowning around during choir practice—or, most of all, teasing Mary Beth Harvey. Of course, Travis gets his comeuppance: he's been cho-

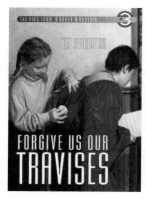

sen to sing the solo during the dedication service for the renovated church building, a prospect that both terrifies and pleases him. This time, however, he'll have to be on his best behavior, which means he's a perfect target for Mary Beth's revenge and in for an uproarious finale.

Ages 7–10 • Grades 3–5 • ISBN 0-88995-207-8 paper • 10 B&W line drawings • CDN 6.95 • US 4.95 • UK £3.99

Second Banana

Ryan Sweeney is the uncertain accomplice of the notorious Travis Bee, school prankster. Ryan doesn't really have any close friends, and he wonders whether Travis may be someone to team up with. But Travis's practical jokes are unpredictable, and Ryan soon discovers that even a trusted accomplice can be the victim of Travis's shenanigans. Ryan doesn't

want to be Travis's second banana, but who else will buddy up with him? It's not always easy to fit in. What Ryan needs is some confidence in his own talents, and he's about to discover them in ways he never imagined.

Ages 7–10 • Grades 3–5 • ISBN 0-88995-241-8 paper • 10 B&W line drawings • CDN 6.95 • US 4.95 • UK £3.99

About the Author

Ted Staunton is a highly celebrated comic novelist for children and is well known for his Green Applestreet Gang series as well as for several picture books, including *Puddleman* and *Simon's Surprise.* His novels for young adults include the Cyril and Maggie series, his new Morgan series and *Hope Springs a Leak,* which was nominated for the Hackmatack Children's Choice Book Award and for the Silver Birch Award. The Monkey Mountain Books are his first series for young readers.

Since 1985 Ted Staunton has divided his time between writing and a busy schedule as a speaker, workshop leader, storyteller and musical performer for children and adults. He lives in Port Hope with his wife, Melanie Browne, and his son, Will.